STORY AND ART BY

NORIYUKI KONISHI

ORIGINAL CONCEPT AND SUPERVISED BY LEVEL-5 INC.

# YO-KAI WATCH™

## Volume 21

VIZ Media Edition

**Story and Art by Noriyuki Konishi**
**Original Concept and Supervised by LEVEL-5 Inc.**

Translation/Tetsuichiro Miyaki
English Adaptation/Aubrey Sitterson
Lettering/John Hunt
Design/Kam Li
Editor/Megan Bates



Printed in the U.S.A.

Published by VIZ Media, LLC
P.O. Box 77010
San Francisco, CA 94107

10 9 8 7 6 5 4 3 2 1
First printing, May 2023

STORY AND ART BY

NORIYUKI KONISHI

ORIGINAL CONCEPT AND SUPERVISED BY LEVEL-5 INC.

# CHARACTER INTRODUCTION

## NATE ADAMS

AN ORDINARY ELEMENTARY SCHOOL STUDENT UNTIL WHISPER GAVE HIM THE YO-KAI WATCH, AND HE'S USED IT TO MAKE A BUNCH OF YO-KAI FRIENDS!

## WHISPER

A YO-KAI BUTLER FREED BY NATE, WHISPER USES HIS EXTENSIVE KNOWLEDGE TO TEACH HIM ALL ABOUT YO-KAI!

## JIBANYAN

A CAT WHO BECAME A YO-KAI WHEN HE PASSED AWAY. HE IS FRIENDLY, CAREFREE, AND THE FIRST YO-KAI THAT NATE BEFRIENDED. HE'S BEEN TRYING TO FIGHT TRUCKS, BUT HE ALWAYS LOSES.

**BARNABY BERNSTEIN**

NATE'S CLASSMATE.
NICKNAME: BEAR.
CAN BE MISCHIEVOUS.

**EDWARD ARCHER**

NATE'S CLASSMATE.
NICKNAME: EDDIE.
HE ALWAYS WEARS
HEAPHONES.

**KATIE FORESTER**

THE MOST POPULAR
GIRL IN NATE'S CLASS.

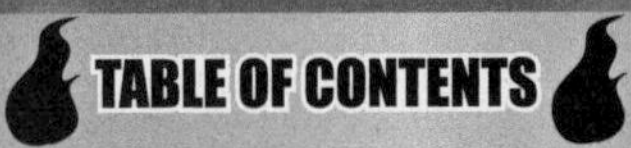
TABLE OF CONTENTS

CHAPTER 221
VACUUM YO-KAI
URNFULFILLED

IT'S BEEN A LONG TIME SINCE I GOT SUCH A BAD GRADE...

Integers and Decimals
Nathan Adams
3
Answer the following questions.
1.435m
What decimal place is 5 in 1.435
14.35 is 1.435 multiplied by what?
using an equation.
Fill in the empty box.
Solve the following equations

HOW DID YOU MANAGE TO ONLY GET THREE POINTS OUT OF 100?
HOW DID I DO IT?

THAT'S EASY! ♪ I DIDN'T STUDY AND ANSWERED ALL THE QUESTIONS WITH WILD GUESSES! ♪
Yeesh...
YEAH, I FIGURED AS MUCH.

WHAT AM I GOING TO DO?! IF I SHOW THIS TO MY MOM...
...SHE'S NOT GOING TO LET ME WATCH TV OR PLAY VIDEO GAMES OR EVEN READ COMICS!
YOU'LL JUST HAVE TO APOLOGIZE.
LOOK AT THIS! LOOK AT IT!
C'MON! A GRADE THIS BAD? APOLOGIZING CAN'T FIX THIS!
WHY IS HE SO ANGRY?

THEN WHY DON'T YOU JUST GET RID OF IT?
DESTROY THE EVIDENCE. ♪
!
...

WHAT ARE YOU TALKING ABOUT?!
GETTING RID OF IT IS THE COWARD'S WAY OUT! IT'S NOT BRAVE OR STRONG!
I'D RATHER HIDE IT SOMEWHERE IT'LL NEVER BE FOUND THAN GET RID OF IT!
HOW IS THAT ANY DIFFERENT ?!
I don't get it.
HIDING THE TEST WON'T SOLVE ANYTHING!
THE ONLY THING YOU CAN DO NOW IS STUDY HARD AND DO BETTER ON THE NEXT TEST!

ARE YOU EVEN LISTENING TO ME?!

FWUMP

HMM... WHERE SHOULD I HIDE IT?

BAAM

MEET THE YO-KAI URNFUL-FILLED. ♪

YOU DON'T NORMALLY INTRODUCE ME TO YO-KAI, WHISPER. ♪

NICE TO MEET--
FWOOSH
AIYEEEEE! MY HEAD GOT SUCKED INTO MY STOMACH!
HIS HEAD ?!

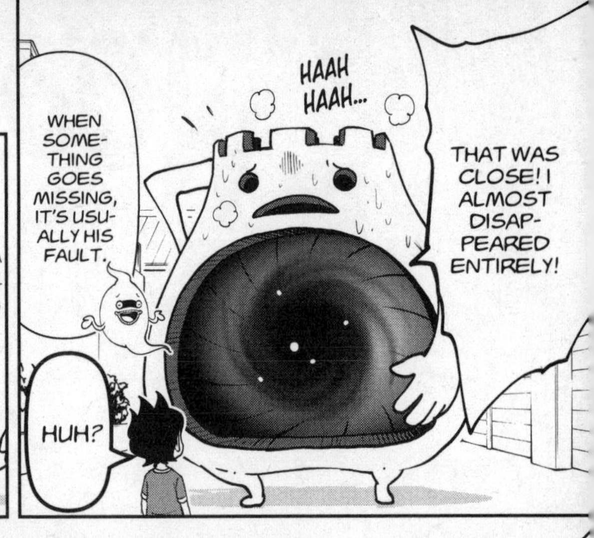
HAAH HAAH...
THAT WAS CLOSE! I ALMOST DISAP-PEARED ENTIRELY!
HUH?
WHEN SOME-THING GOES MISSING, IT'S USU-ALLY HIS FAULT.

BOW
I'M SO SORRY !!
WHAT A SUPER ANNOY-ING YO-KAI!

FWOOSH
AHHHH! I'M GETTING SUCKED INSIDE AGAIN!
THAT'S ENOUGH!

Oh, an empty can!
LATELY HE'S BEEN HELPING HUMANS OUT BY PICKING UP GARBAGE.
...

SNIFF...
KLAK KLAK KLAK

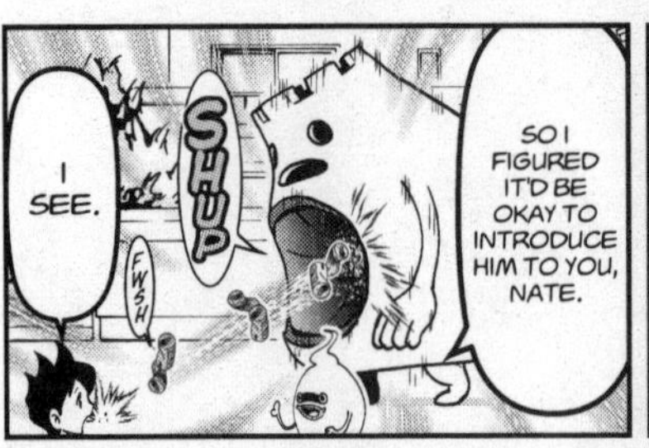
SO I FIGURED IT'D BE OKAY TO INTRODUCE HIM TO YOU, NATE.
SHUP
FWSH
I SEE.

I MET A YO-KAI WHO SCOLDED ME FOR WHAT I WAS DOING...

I PROMISED THAT YO-KAI...

...THAT I WOULD START HELPING HUMANS.

WOW, THAT MUST HAVE BEEN A NICE YO-KAI YOU MET. ♪

NO MATTER HOW MUCH I ABSORB, I'M NEVER FULL...

I'LL SUCK YOU IN TOO!

BEFORE YOU ABSORB ME, I'M GONNA BEAT THE LIVING DAYLIGHTS OUT OF YOU!

AWWW...

CAN YOU JUST ABSORB THE GARBAGE?

I'LL DO JUST THAT.

OH, I'D NEVER EAT A VEHICLE. I JUST ABSORBED IT.

EVERYTHING I ABSORB BELONGS TO ME! EVERYTHING I'VE EVER ABSORBED BELONGS TO ME!

THAT'S A TERRIBLE WAY TO LOOK AT THINGS!

CHECK IT OUT IN VOL. 16!

WHAT HAPPENS TO THE THINGS YOU SUCK UP?
I DON'T KNOW THAT. BUT...
NOTHING I SUCK IN WILL EVER RETURN.
THAT'S SCARY...

IN THAT CASE, NATE PROBABLY WON'T PUT HIS TEST IN...
...
IF IT NEVER COMES BACK, THAT'S THE SAME AS GETTING RID OF IT...
RIGHT.

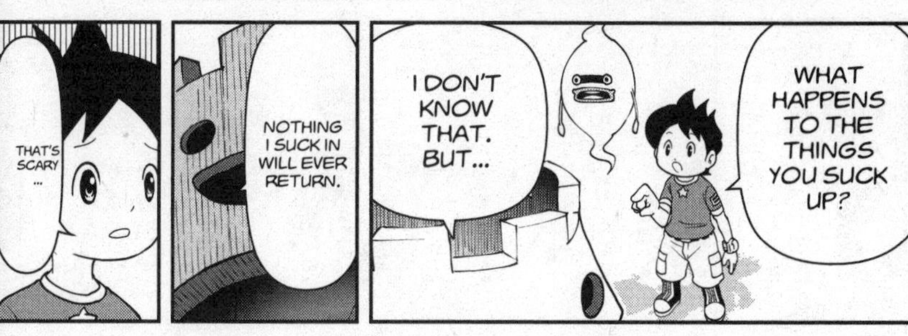

NONCHALANT

EH, I DON'T CARE ANYMORE. ♪

*Suck this in, please!*

*WHAT WAS ALL THAT ABOUT, THEN?!*

IT'S COWARDLY TO...

...GET RID OF IT!

HEY, NATE, WHAT ARE YOU DOING?

B-BMP

NATE'S MOM!

HUH?

YO-KAI ARE INVISIBLE TO THE HUMAN EYE.

OH!

?

WHAT'S THIS?

NOOOOO!

I'M DONE FOR!

OH.

SHOOM

WAY TO GO, WHISPER!

HEY...
SHAA
ZWOOSH
WHISPER!!
ZWOOSH
?
SPIT HIM BACK OUT, URNFUL-FILLED!
NO CAN DO.
NOTHING I SUCK IN WILL EVER RETURN.

WHAT'S THE MATTER, NATE?

OH, UH... NOTHING...

ZWOOSH

COME ON, LET'S GO HOME.

HELP ME...

GRRP...

WOW! YOU'RE FLYING FAST ENOUGH TO NOT GET SUCKED IN!

FWIP

FWIP

GWOOSH
DON'T WORRY! I'M PROTECTING YOUR HORRIBLE TEST GRADE WITH MY LIFE!
SHEFF
SHEFF
WHAT?! STOP DOING THAT! HANG IN THERE, I'LL HELP YOU!

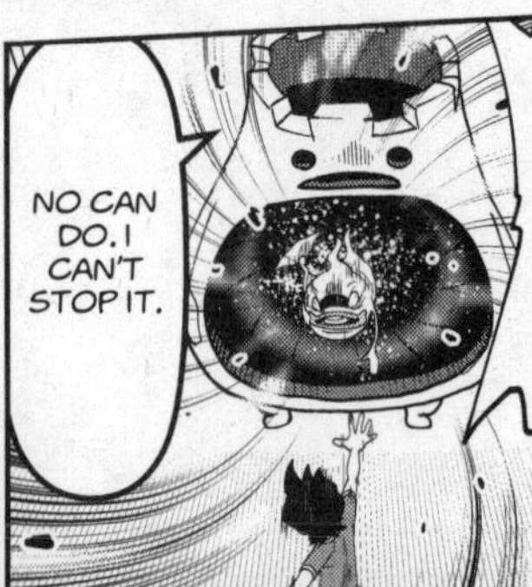

URNFUL-FILLED, STOP SUCKING WHISPER IN!
NO CAN DO. I CAN'T STOP IT.

GRAB HOLD OF ME, WHISPER!

UUUGH!

I'LL SAVE YOU NO MATTER WHAT!
NAAAAATE!
...!!
AHHHHH!!
SWIP
SHOOM
SHUP
GRAB
DON'T WORRY, I'LL PULL YOU OUT!!
THANKS!
GRRP...
HRRRRNGH!
YOU CAN DO IT!
URRRRGH!
GRRP...

AIYEEEE! MY ARMS GOT SUCKED IN!
KRRRCH
TUUUG
HEY...
HRRRRNGH!
ARRRRGH!
SHUUUP
YAYY! EVERY-THING'S FINE NOW!
THANKS, URNFUL-FILLED!
...
EVERY-THING WASN'T FINE FOR NATE.
YOU SHOULDN'T HIDE THINGS FROM YOUR PARENTS.

CHAPTER 222
UNCARING YO-KAI
OH WHEEL
WHUNGK
ZZZ...
DEFEATED AGAIN, HUH?
JIBANYAN
A YO-KAI WHOSE DREAM IS TO DEFEAT A TRUCK.
SKRRRRRCH
PLOP
!
OH NO! I FELL ASLEEP AT THE WHEEL AND HIT A CAT!
WHAT SHOULD I DO ?!
VROOM
!
...
WHAT?! YOU CAN SEE JIBAN-YAN?!
WHO ARE YOU ?!

VRROOM
OH WHEEL...
TWCH TWCH...
COME BACK HERE!

GET AWAY FROM ME, MONSTER!
VRROOM
THUNGK
ARRRRGH!
OH NO, I GOT SO SCARED I RAN INTO IT...
SKRRCH
WHAT SHOULD I DO?!
OH WHEEL, IT'S JUST A MONSTER!
VROOM
TWCH TWCH
HEY...
SHUP
OWWW...
WHAT?! THE CAT'S STILL ALIVE!
SKRRRRCH
I'M SO SORRY! I'LL TAKE YOU TO THE HOSPITAL!
HOLD ON! BACKING-ING UP!

VROOOM
SPLUBT
HEEEEEY!
WHOOPS...
?
WHAT?!
YOU'RE NOT A CAT OR A MONSTER... YOU'RE...
...A YO-KAI?!
THAT'S GREAT! ♪
WHY IS THAT GREAT?! APOLOGIZE FOR RUNNING INTO ME!
MEOW?! A CAR YO-KAI?!
E BEST FRESH
HE FISH PL
I REMEMBER NOW! YOU'RE A YO-KAI WHO DOESN'T CARE ABOUT ANYTHING...
OH WHEEL!
HONK HONK
UNCARING YO-KAI
OH WHEEL
Yeeaah!
YOU JUST COMMITTED A HIT-AND-RUN! TWO OF THEM!
HOW RUDE! I DID NOT!
FISH PLACE

I JUST DIDN'T CARE ABOUT IT!
HUFF HUFF
HONK HONK
THAT DOESN'T CHANGE ANY-THING!

FRESH FISH
LIVE FISH
THE FISH PLACE
OH WHEEL... ♪
Bye!
VROOM
THAT'S EXACTLY WHAT I'M TALKING ABOUT! YOU SHOULD SHOW MORE CONCERN!
A CAR YO-KAI? THAT'S PERFECT! ♪
?
YOU'RE RIGHT!
FRESH
FISH PLACE
WHAT?! YOU FIGHT AGAINST VEHICLES?!
HELP ME WITH MY TRAIN-ING!
BUT YOU'LL DIE!
DON'T WORRY ABOUT IT!
!!

VRROOM
OH WHEEL. ♪
EVEN IF YOU DIE, IT WON'T BOTHER ME! ♪
THAT'S TERRIBLE ...
HERE I COME! ♪
Paws of Fury!
CHOOK CHOOK
YAAH!
!
YOU THINK YOU CAN JUST CRUSH ME?! I'LL ATTACK YOUR UNDER-CARRIAGE!
SHA
CHOOK CHOOK CHOOK CHOOK CHOOK CHOOK

WHAAAAAT?!
OH WHEEL BEAT YOU WITH A PUNCH!
YOU HAVE TO FIGHT ME LIKE AN ORDINARY CAR...
SORRY...
TWCH TWCH
OH WHEEL... ♪ WHAT-EVER!
VRROOM
...

CHAPTER 223
SORE THROAT YO-KAI COUGHKOFF
THE BEST FRESH FISH
LIVE FISH
FRESH
THE FISH PLACE
KOFF KOFF
MY THROAT FEELS TINGLY.
AHHH AHHH...
HKKH HKKH
ARE YOU SICK?
You should wear a mask...
DO YOU THINK YOU COULD HAVE CAUGHT A COLD SOMEWHERE?
I DON'T SEE HOW...
COUGHKOFF
HMMM
I DON'T SEE THE YO-KAI COUGHKOFF AROUND...

ZZZ...
ZZZ...
YESTERDAY I TOOK A NAP IN THE SNOW WITH MY MOUTH OPEN...
In the middle of winter?!
THAT'S WHY YOU'RE SICK!

IF IT'S JUST AN ORDINARY COLD...
TUG
TUG
...
...THERE MUST BE GERMS IN MY THROAT!

I'LL RIP THEM OUT!!
SHUP
YOU CAN'T GRAB GERMS WITH YOUR HAND, MUCH LESS PULL THEM OUT!

MEOW?!

WAIT... DID YOU ACTUALLY DO IT? DID YOU GRAB HOLD OF A GERM?!
TUUUG...

BAARRF

URRRRGH! I SHOVED MY HAND IN TOO FAR...

NATURALLY.

SPLUBT

POPT
HE CAUGHT IT AND PULLED IT OUT!
And it's all slimy!
WHAAAAT?!
GASP GASP
WHAT? YOU COULDN'T GET OUT ON YOUR OWN?
THANK YOU FOR PULLING ME OUT!
HEFF, HEFF ...
PHEW! I'VE BEEN STUCK IN YOUR THROAT THIS ENTIRE TIME...
COUGHKOFF
YOUR THROAT FEELS ITCHY WHEN IT INSPIRITS YOU.

I WAS HALF ASLEEP WHEN I ACCIDENTALLY FELL INTO JIBANYAN'S MOUTH YESTERDAY...

ZZZ...

POPT

YEAH, THAT HAPPENS ALL THE TIME. ♪

WHAT?! NO, IT DOESN'T!

ANY-WAY, I'M GRATE-FUL FOR BOTH OF YOU.

BUT MY THROAT STILL HURTS...

HA HA, THAT MUST BE FROM ALL THE BLOOD MY SPIKES DREW! ♪

GRAB

GRAB

DON'T "HA HA" ME!

APOLOGIZE!

THUNGK

AHHHHH!

SPLUBT
...
HE'S STUCK ON MY HEAD!
HOW DOES HE KEEP MAKING IT WORSE?
AHHH
HHHH!
I DON'T GET IT. IF YOU TWO FUSE TOGETH-ER...
...YOU SHOULD TURN INTO THORNYAN...
FUSION
THORNYAN
ZZT ZZT
YOU'RE RIGHT...

FUSION!

CHOMP

AIIIIE!

WHAT KIND OF FUSION IS THAT?!

GULP

SWIP

SWIP

SPLUBT
AHHHH! IT HURTS!
He's stuck in my mouth!
THAT'S NO SURPRISE...

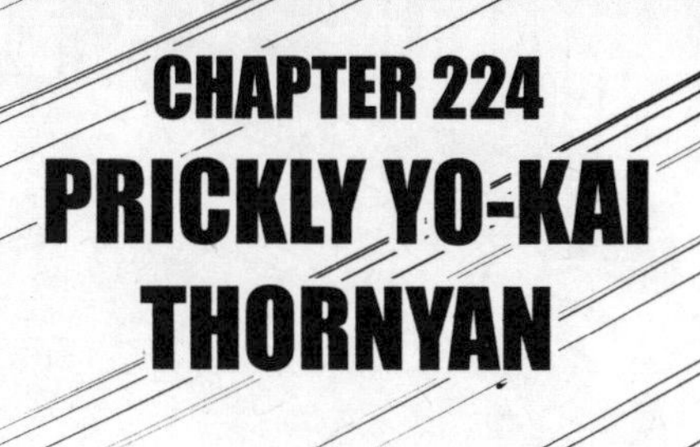

# CHAPTER 224
# PRICKLY YO-KAI THORNYAN

FWEEEE

BRRRRR, IT'S FREEZ-ING!

LET'S GO HOME AND WARM UP...

SHUDDER SHUDDER

TRRMBLL TRRMBLL

RIGHT.

IT'S NOT THAT COLD! I CAN'T BELIEVE YOU GUYS!
BAM
HEY, JIBAN-YAN! IT'S BEEN A WHILE! ♪
I DON'T REMEM-BER YOU BEING SO TOL-ERANT OF THE COLD THOUGH.

CATS AREN'T TOLERANT OF THE COLD.
PRICKLE PRICKLE
I'M JUST STRON-GER THAN YOU.
THORNYAN!!
CAN'T YOU TAKE A HINT?
PRICKLE PRICKLE
YAP YAP
COME ON! HOW LONG HAVE YOU KNOWN ME?
SORRY...
THORNYAN
A PRICKLY YO-KAI WHO SAYS MEAN, PRICKLY THINGS.
WAIT... THAT MEANS THAT YO-KAI IS SOME-WHERE AROUND HERE TOO!
YOU'RE RIGHT!

BINGO.

TA-DAAAH

OWWWW! DON'T COME OUT!

IT'S IN HIS MOUTH!

SHUKT SHUKT SHUKT

COUGHKOFF
A YO-KAI THAT MAKES YOUR THROAT ITCHY.

WHEN JIBANYAN AND COUGHKOFF FUSE...
...THEY TURN INTO THORN-YAN.

I'LL SMASH INTO YOU...

CHOOM

CHOOM

THORN THWACK!!

I TAUGHT YOU A LESSON BEFORE, BUT I GUESS THAT WASN'T ENOUGH!

OH NO! I LEARNED MY LESSON. IT'S JUST THAT...

BUT YOU'RE THE ONE SPREADING ALL THE GERMS AROUND!

HAVE YOU LOST YOUR MIND?!

WHAT WOULD YOU DO IF I CAME DOWN WITH SOMETHING?!

WHAAAT!

AAAAA ARRGH! MY EYE!

SHUKT

YOU'RE IN HIS MOUTH TO KEEP WARM ?!
...IT'S SO COLD TODAY.
SHIVER SHIVER
FWEEEE

NO! IF I DON'T FUSE WITH HIM...
TRRMBLL TRRMBLL
SHUDDER SHUDDER
TRRMBLL TRRMBLL
SHUDDER SHUDDER
YOU'RE BEING SO SELFISH!

SHUT IT, JIBANYAN! IT'S COLD OUT THERE!
SHUDDER SHUDDER
TRRMBLL TRRMBLL

OWWWW!

TRRMBL TRRMBL

SHUDDER SHUDDER

...I'LL END UP CAUSING EVEN MORE TROUBLE BY TREM-BLING.

HE'S SHAKING AND THE THORNS ARE STABBING JIBANYAN'S MOUTH!!

SHIVER SHIVER

SHIVER SHIVER

SHUDDER SHUDDER

SHIVER SHIVER

SHIVER SHIVER

SHIVER SHIVER

NAH, I'M FINE INSIDE HIS MOUTH...
I WAS TRYING TO BE NICE! YOU'RE BEING A NUISANCE IN THERE!
FWEEEE
IT'S SO... COLD...
IT'S FREEZ-ING TODAY...
SHUDDER SHUDDER
AH...
...CHOO!
AHHH!
HE CAME OUT!
POPT
PHEW! I DID IT... BUT IT'S SO COLD...
YOU'VE TURNED BACK INTO JIBANYAN! ♪
OKAY, I'M GOING TO TEACH THIS GUY A LESSON! WHISPER, WHICH YOKAI WOULD BE ABLE TO BEAT HIM?
HUH?

SHUKT

...

SORRY...

SHOCK

HE GOT STUCK THERE WHEN YOU SNEEZED...

WHY ARE YOU TRYING TO SQUEEZE INTO MY MOUTH?!
IZZGH!!
SHOVE
SHOVE
YOU'RE NOTHING LIKE COLD-HEARTED JIBANYAN.
STAAARE
SHF SHF
Not again...

HEY, WOULDN'T IT BE EASIER IF YOU JUST MOVED YOUR BODY TO WARM UP?!
ARRRGH!
IN THAT CASE, I HAVE NO CHOICE... I HAVE TO FORCE MYSELF INTO YOUR MOUTH!

...

HOW COULD YOU THINK I WOULDN'T NOTICE ?!
FWEEE
OH... YOU NOTICED.
TRRMBL TRRMBL
SHIVER SHIVER

THAT'S TOO MUCH WORK.
I don't want to bother.
IT'S WAY MORE WORK TO TRY AND SQUEEZE INTO SOME-ONE'S MOUTH!
IT'S FREEZING OUT HERE AND I'VE HAD ENOUGH OF YOU.
FWOOO
SHIVER SHIVER
TRRMBL TRRMBL
LET'S JUST GET RID OF HIM AND GO HOME.
!!
RIGHT.
GET RID OF ME?

TAKE THIS! PAWS OF FURY!!
CHOOM
CHOOM
CHOOM
DID YOU FORGET ABOUT MY PRICKLY BODY?
CHOOM
CHOOM
CHOOM
CHOOM
CHOOM
IF YOU PUNCH IT, YOU'RE THE ONE WHO'S GOING TO SUFFER!
I DON'T EVEN NEED TO DODGE!
CHOOM
SHFF
SHFF
SHFF
HA HA HA, YOU'RE NOT EVEN HIT-TING...
HUH ...?

AHH! THE PUNCHES ARE FANNING COLD AIR ON ME!
IT'S SO COLD!
FWEEE
FWEEE
SHIVER SHIVER
SHIVER SHIVER
SHUDDER SHUDDER
SHUDDER SHUDDER
FWEEE
YOU'RE SO WEAK AGAINST THE COLD!
THUD
I HAVE TO HIDE!
NOT AGAIN!
Hmmph!
SH-
SHA
AS I EXPECTED, YOU TRIED TO ESCAPE INTO WHISPER'S MOUTH!
YOU WERE MISSING ME ON PUR-POSE!
!!

PAWS OF FURY !!!
CHOOM! CHOOM! CHOOM!
AIYEEEEE!
HE'S USING WHISPER'S BODY TO SHIELD HIS PUNCHES FROM THE SPIKES!
URGH!
WHISPER, ARE YOU OKAY?!

HNNGH

DO I LOOK... OKAY... TO YOU?

TWCH TWCH...

NO, SORRY...

HEY, COUGH-KOFF! COME OUT!

...

PANT PANT

UGH...IT'S SO COLD THAT I DON'T WANT TO GO OUTSIDE. BUT AT THIS RATE...

HE'S GOING TO DEFEAT ME EVEN WITH WHISPER BETWEEN US!

I'LL JUMP OUT AND PIERCE JIBANYAN WHEN HE GETS CLOSE!

BAM

YOU'LL BE SORRY FOR NOT COMING OUT!

NOW!

SHA

!!

!!

SHUKT

AGH... I'M STUCK!

AVOID LETTING GERMS GET IN YOUR MOUTH. WEAR A MASK.
HNNGH
TWCH TWCH
WHISPER!
S-SORRY ...
HNGH...

## BONUS COMIC ①

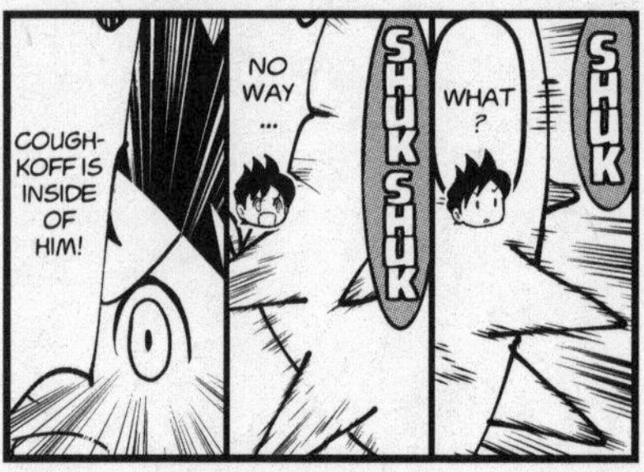

# CHAPTER 225
# POPULARITY YO-KAI CUPISTOL

ORDINARY ELEMENTARY SCHOOL STUDENT
**NATE ADAMS**
(HE'S THE GUY WHO'S ON THE COVER.)

...
KATIE'S JUST AS CUTE AS EVER! ♡

H-HYUK HYUK HYUK... ♪
NATE?
Your eyes look weird...

I WANT TO GET CLOSER TO HER. ♡
I WANT TO HOLD HER HAND AND WALK HER HOME. ♡
...
WHY DON'T YOU ASK DAN-DOODLE FOR HELP?
NO WAY. BEING POPULAR IS MEANING-LESS IF IT'S BECAUSE OF A YO-KAI.
AND I END UP LOOK-ING LIKE A TOTALLY DIFFER-ENT GUY ANYWAY.
NO...
...

BAAAM
YEEAAH!
I WANT TO BE POPULAR BECAUSE OF MY OWN CHARMING PERSONALITY!
IF YOU AREN'T ALREADY POPULAR, THAT MEANS YOU MUST NOT BE ATTRACTIVE.
What are you standing on?
...

WASN'T THERE A YO-KAI THAT MADE ME ATTRACTIVE ?!
YOU'RE ALREADY GIVING UP ON NOT USING A YO-KAI ?!
KRCH

THIS ONE!

YO-KAI WATCH
A DEVICE THAT LETS YOU SEE YO-KAI.
YO-KAI MEDAL
A MEDAL GIVEN TO YOU BY THE YO-KAI YOU BEFRIEND.

YO-KAI MEDAL! DO YOUR THING!

BY PLACING THE MEDAL INTO THE YO-KAI WATCH, YOU CAN SUMMON A YO-KAI.

CALL-ING...

VRRVRR

CUPISTOL!

CUPISTOL
ANYONE IT SHOOTS WITH ITS HEART-SHAPED PISTOL WILL FALL IN LOVE WITH THE PERSON WHO REQUESTED IT!

I WANT TO BE POPULAR WITH GIRLS!

NO PROB-LEM! ♪

*WHAT HAPPENED TO ALL THAT TALK ABOUT YOUR OWN CHARM?*

PIECE OF CAKE. JUST LEAVE IT TO ME! ♪
DID YOU HAVE SOMEONE SPECIFIC IN MIND?
OF COURSE! KATIE, PLEASE!

HEY, NATE! WHAT'S UP?
!
CLASSMATE KATIE FORESTER
...
...

AHHHHHHHHH!

NOOO-OOOO!! I FORGOT I WAS IN THE CLASSROOM!

HOW COULD YOU FORGET THAT?

PSST

HE WAS SAYING SOMETHING ABOUT KATIE TOO.

PSST PSST

AND SOMETHING ABOUT HIS OWN PERSONAL CHARM ...

HE'S BEEN SHOUTING THAT HE WANTS TO BE POPULAR.

SO WEIRD!

...

EWW, CREEPY ...

MURMUR MURMUR

KATIE ...

GOOD-BYE...

WHAT ?!

!

I DON'T SEE ANYTHING WRONG...

...WITH BEING HONEST ABOUT YOUR FEEL- INGS.

...
BECAUSE HE'S ALWAYS TALKING TO YO-KAI!
AND I'M USED TO NATE TALKING TO HIMSELF! ♪

I GOT IT!
KAAATIEEEEEE. ♡

YOU SHOT KATIE, DIDN'T YOU, CUPISTOL?! ♪
THAT'S IT! ♪ THANKS, CUPISTOL!
...
I HAVEN'T SHOT ANYONE YET.
I WAS HAVING FUN WATCHING YOU FREAK OUT AND FORGOT!
YOU DIDN'T SHOOT HER?
WHAT ...?
TH-TH-TH-THEN ...
KATIE IS ACTUALLY STANDING UP FOR ME BECAUSE SHE WANTS TO?!
I GUESS SO.
...

KATIE HAS FALLEN FOR MY CHARMS!

YAAAHOOO!

...
...

KATIE, DON'T LET HIM TRICK YOU.
...
HE'S SCAR-ING ME.
OH NO ...

NATE'S LOSING IT.
NOOOOO! I FORGOT I WAS IN THE CLASSROOM AGAIN!

KATIE MIGHT CHANGE HER MIND IF THE OTHER GIRLS KEEP TALKING!
I'M SORRY, BUT I CAN'T LET THEM GET IN THE WAY!
CALLING ...
HELLO. ♪
...WAZZAT!!
WAZZAT
A YO-KAI THAT MAKES PEOPLE FORGET THINGS.
I NEED YOU TO ERASE EVERY-ONE'S MEMORIES FROM THE LAST FIVE MINUTES!
CHOMP
CHOMP
NO PROBLEM! ♪

HUH? WHAT WAS I JUST DOING?

?

?

THANKS, WAZZAT. ♪

WHAT HAPPENED TO WANTING TO BE POPULAR BECAUSE OF YOUR OWN CHARM?
...
SHUP
WAIT... WHAT?
NEVER MIND.

HEY, KATIE ...

THANK YOU FOR STANDING UP FOR ME. ♪

!

W-WHAT ARE YOU TALKING ABOUT?

YOU'RE BEING REALLY WEIRD.

I WIPED HER MEMORY CLEAN JUST LIKE YOU ASKED! ♪

CUPI-
STOL,
SHOOT
KATIE!
WHAT?! SHOOT KATIE?!
OH NO! I FORGOT I WAS IN THE CLASSROOM AGAIN!
WAZZAT, ERASE ALL OF MY MEMORIES!
...
KATIE AVOIDED HIM FOR A WHILE AFTER THAT.

## BONUS COMIC ②

CHAPTER 226
STICKY YO-KAI
QUAGMIRA

OKAY! LET'S CLIMB TO THE TOP!
YEEAAAH!
EDDIE
NATE'S CLASSMATE
BEAR
NATE'S CLASSMATE
KATIE
NATE'S CLASSMATE
NATE ADAMS
AN ORDINARY ELEMENTARY SCHOOL STUDENT
WE'LL EAT OUR LUNCHES AT THE PEAK WHILE LOOK-ING OUT AT THE TOWN!
YEEAAH!

GASP!
GASP!

HEY! HURRY UP, NATE!
STAGGER STAGGER...
TREMBLE TREMBLE...
ARE YOU OKAY?
SORRY... MY LEGS FEEL...SO HEAVY!

WHOO-AAA! IT'S STICKING TO ME LIKE GLUE!

ARE YOU SURPRISED IT'S ANOTHER YO-KAI?

WHAT'S WRONG, NATE?! WAS THERE A SNAKE OR SOMETHING?!
AHH! IT'S NOTHING! GO ON AHEAD!

WE CAN'T LEAVE YOU ALONE IN THE MOUNTAINS.
HE'S RIGHT. LET'S TAKE A BREAK.
...

SHUDDER......

NO, SERI-OUSLY... GO...!

I'LL BE FINE...

STAARE

PLEASE... JUST GO...

I NEED TO GET RID OF THIS GUY! AND FAST!

YO-KAI ARE INVISIBLE TO THE HUMAN EYE.

AND THEY CALL THEMSELVES YOUR FRIENDS?

GLOOM

I feel so sorry for you.

IT'S BECAUSE YOU'RE INSPIRITING ME!

OH.

YOU'VE GOT TO BE KID-DING!

I really appreciate it! ♪

I HANG ON TO PEOPLE BECAUSE IT'S EASIER FOR ME TO MOVE AROUND!

C'mon, help me out! ♪

WHAT DO YOU MEAN KIDDING ?!

!!

HA HA HA HA♪
WELL, I GUESS I MAY AS WELL JUST KEEP CLINGING TO PEOPLE THEN. ♪
NO! THAT'S NOT WHAT I'M SAYING AT ALL!

STICKY YO-KAI QUAGMIRA

OKAY, FIRST YOUR RIGHT FOOT...
HUP.
TUG!!

NOW THE LEFT ONE...
...
TUG...
...
Okay, right, left, right...
TUG
TMP
TUG
TUP

I CAN'T KEEP DOING THIS! IT'S EXHAUSTING!
CURSES!
THEN STOP DOING IT!

WAIT!
I KNOW WHO CAN DRIVE THIS YO-KAI AWAY!
FWIP

CALLING...
VNNNN

...SWELTON!!
VRRRN
I'LL GET RID OF YOU WITH SWEAT!
WOW! GREAT IDEA!
SWELTON
YOU CAN'T STOP SWEATING WHEN HE INSPIRITS YOU.
HA HA HA. ♪
NICE TRY, BUT I CAN STILL CLING TO YOUR CLOTHES! ♪
Oh no...
SHOCK
RIGHT...
WHOA! WHAT THE HECK?!
HE'S SO SLIPPERY!
ZLLLSH
SLIP SLIP SLIP
WHAT?
HUH?

FWUMP

WHAAAAA?!

MY CLOTHES SLIPPED OFF BECAUSE OF THE SWEAT TOO!

SWIP

I DIDN'T WANT TO GET INTO A FIGHT WITH YOU...

...BUT NOT BEING ABLE TO MOVE AROUND IS TERRIBLE!

THAT SAID, YOUR POWER COULD COME IN HANDY DEPENDING ON HOW YOU USE IT!
Thanks for your help!
...

LIKE IN-SPIRITING SOME-ONE WHO IS RUNNING AWAY AFTER DOING SOME-THING BAD! ♪
!

ME... CATCH BAD PEOPLE ?!
YEAH!
SOUNDS GOOD, RIGHT? ♪

NAH, NO THANKS. BAD GUYS RUN AWAY TOO QUICKLY FOR ME. ♪

NO, NO, NO, NO, NO, NO.

SHF SHF

SOME PEOPLE WILL COME UP WITH ANY EXCUSE TO AVOID BEING USEFUL...

If I ran after someone like that, I'd get all sweaty and tired.
DON'T EXPECT QUAGMIRA TO TURN OVER A NEW LEAF. THE ONLY THING THEY CAN DO IS HOLD PEOPLE DOWN...
UH-HUH...

NAAAAATE!
!

HEY, KATIE! ♪

I CAME BACK BECAUSE I WAS WORRIED ABOUT YOU.

ARE YOU ALL--
YEAH, I'M--
WHAT?

AGH!

AHHHHHH!

SHA

AHHHHHHH!

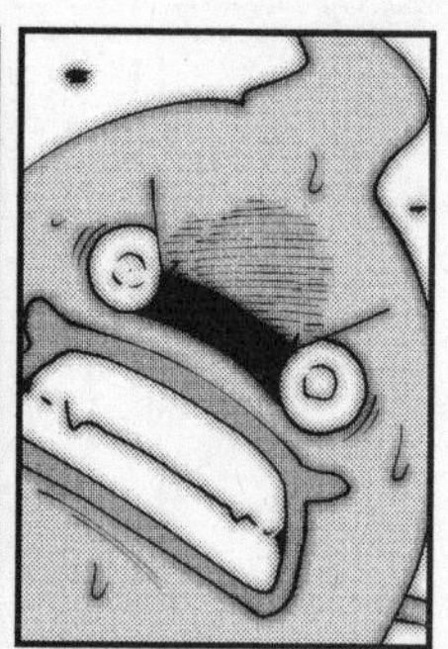

EEEEEEEEEEEEEK!

AHH HH!

I'M A YO-KAI, SO SHE CAN SEE RIGHT THROUGH ME!

YO-KAI ARE INVISIBLE TO THE HUMAN EYE.

NO! NO! IT'S NOT WHAT YOU THINK, KATIE!

DAAAASH

...

GLARE

LEAVE IT TO ME!

?!

GRRRP

YOU'RE GOING TO GO TELL EVERYONE THERE'S A NAKED WEIRDO HERE, RIGHT?! I WON'T ALLOW IT!

*You're a bad guy!*

WHAT...?! MY LEGS... SO HEAVY...!

OOO

...

KATIE AVOIDED HIM FOR A WHILE AGAIN.
...
STOP THOSE TWO!
WAAH
WAAH
HEY, NATE! ARE YOU OKAY?
NO, LET HER GO! IT'S WORSE FOR HER TO STAY HERE!

CHAPTER 227
DELINQUENT YO-KAI ROUGHRAFF
I'M LATE! I'M LATE!
WHISPER, WHY DIDN'T YOU WAKE ME UP?!
CLOMP CLOMP CLOMP CLOMP CLOMP CLOMP CLOMP
I TRIED!
BUT YOU SAID, "SHUT UP AND LET ME SLEEP! MASTER'S ORDERS!"
REALLY?! I SAID THAT?!
WELL ...

ACTUALLY, I JUST OVER-SLEPT AND THAT'S WHAT I WAS DREAM-ING.
SMAK
RIGHT. THAT... MAKES A LOT MORE SENSE.

YEAH, I GOT A GREAT NIGHT OF SLEEP! ♪
AHHHH! ♪
OH!

KATIE!

KATIE, YOU HAVE TO HURRY OR YOU'LL BE LATE FOR CLASS!
!

YO, NATE.

BAAM

STOP STRESSING ABOUT BEING TARDY.

RULES ARE MADE TO BE BROKEN. ♪
DON'T-YOU-THINK-SO?
...!!

THAT'S A GREAT POINT! ♪ YEAH! ♪
DON'T BE RIDICULOUS! DO YOU REALLY THINK KATIE WOULD SAY THAT?!

...

A YO-KAI!
DUH ...

ROUGHRAFF!
TCH, THERE'S NO TRICK-ING YOU, NATE.
ROUGHRAFF
A YO-KAI THAT WILL TURN ANYONE IT INSPIRITS INTO A DELINQUENT.
OH! HI, NATE.
AHH!
KATIE, YOU'LL BE LATE IF YOU DON'T HURRY!
YO-KAI ARE INVISIBLE TO THE HUMAN EYE.
I FORGOT SOMETHING AT HOME! YOU GO ON AHEAD!
OH, OKAY... BUT YOU SHOULD HURRY TOO!

I DON'T HAVE TIME FOR THIS! IF YOU'RE GOING TO KEEP INSPIRITING PEOPLE, I'LL HAVE TO TEACH YOU A LESSON!
...

OH, NO! I WON'T EVER DO IT AGAIN! I PROMISE!
I'M SO SORRY!
THAT WAS TOO EASY. I BET HE'S JUST SAYING WHAT WE WANT TO HEAR.

NOT BUYING IT, HUH?
Tch.
HE ADMITS IT!
VERY WELL ...
...
!

!!

STARE DOWN!

STARE DOWN

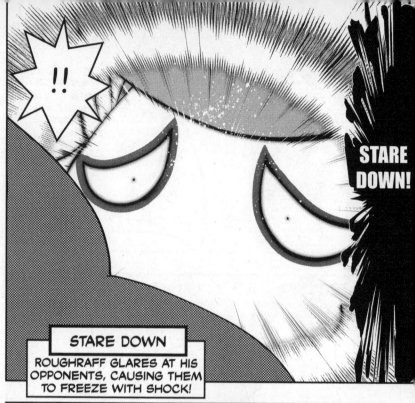

ROUGHRAFF GLARES AT HIS OPPONENTS, CAUSING THEM TO FREEZE WITH SHOCK!

PHEW! I USED WHISPER AS A SHIELD!
TWCH TWCH
SHUDDER SHUDDER
THAT'S TERRIBLE!

DON'T WORRY, WHISPER! I'LL AVENGE YOU!
TWCH TWCH
MAYBE... AN APOLOGY... FIRST?
HUH?
HE'S GONE! COME OUT AND FACE US!
SHFF
TWCH TWCH

NATE, MAY I HAVE A WORD WITH YOU LATER?

...

BA AM

CLOMP CLOMP

HEY, ROUGH-RAFF!

YOU NEED TO STOP INSPIRITING PEOPLE LIKE THIS.

...

YOUR IDEA OF DELIN-QUENTS IS SO OUT OF DATE, IT'S RIDICU-LOUS.

IT WAS THE SAME WHEN YOU INSPIRIT-ED ME!

HONK HONK

YEE AAA AH!

BWAHAHAHA! I'M UN-STOPPABLE! I'LL BEAT THE SNOT OUT OF ANYONE!

THE WHOLE WORLD'S AGAINST ME!

YOU DON'T SEE DELIN-QUENTS LIKE THAT ANYMORE ...

...

...

EH... ROUGH-RAFF?

I DON'T SEE HIM ANY-WHERE... THAT MEANS...

THAT'S WHAT YOU GET FOR ALWAYS LOOKING TO BLAME A YO-KAI!
...
I REALLY APOLO-GIZE!

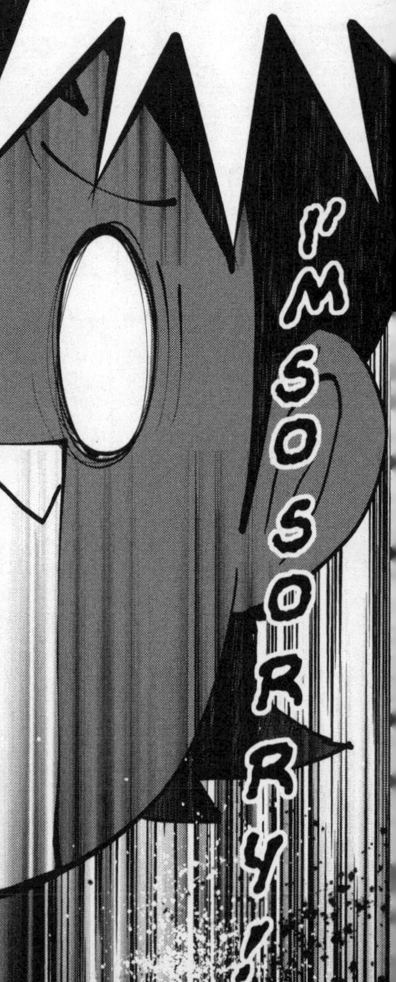
THIS GUY'S THE REAL DEAL!
I'M SO SORRY!

I'M SO VERY SORRY!
HE DODGED MY STARE DOWN WHEN I TRIED TO MAKE A RUN FOR IT, BUT LUCK'S ON MY SIDE! ♪
THIS IS MY CHANCE TO GET OUT OF HERE! ♪

HEY, DON'T WORRY ABOUT IT!
PHEW! HE'S A LOT NICER THAN HE LOOKS! ♪

YOU CAN MAKE IT UP TO ME. WITH CASH. ♪

*How much you got on you, huh?♪*

PAP PAP

NO! HE'S NICE, BUT ALSO TERRIFY-ING!

HEY, I LIKE THAT SOUND! ♪
KRRCH
OH! THAT'S--

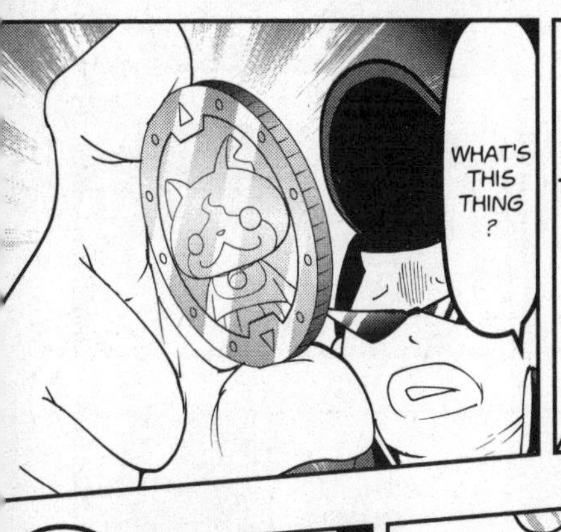

WHAT'S THIS THING?

TOY MEDALS?
GIVE THEM BACK!

I DON'T NEED THESE.

YOU CAN HAVE 'EM!

NO!

...

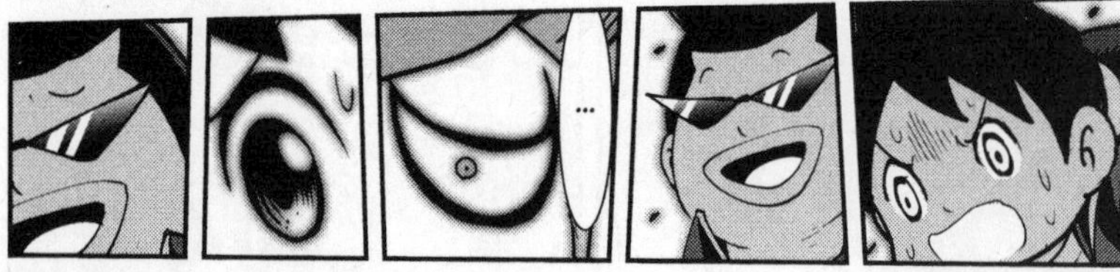

!
SHUP
HUH ?
!

I...I CAN'T MOVE!
SHUDDER SHUDDER
TWCHTWCH
IT'S GUYS LIKE THIS WHO MAKE OTHER DELIN-QUENTS LOOK BAD!
YOU'RE AN EM-BARRASS-MENT TO ALL OF US!
DON'T YOU REALIZE THOSE ARE SIGNS OF FRIENDSHIP? HOW DARE YOU DISRESPECT THEM?!
HE'S NOT GOING ANY-WHERE. GO AHEAD AND BEAT HIM UP, NATE!
URRGH!!
...

WHAT DID YOU... DO TO ME?!

HEY...I CAN'T... MOVE!

TWITCH TWITCH

SHUDDER SHUDDER

WANT ME TO DO IT FOR YOU?

NAW, I DON'T WANT ANYTHING TO DO WITH HIM.

*Let's just leave him here.*

KRCH

...IT'S NOT FAIR TO ATTACK SOMEONE WHO CAN'T MOVE.

ALSO...

URGH... I CAN FINALLY MOVE...

OH... REALLY?

SHOCK

TOO LATE!

ARGH.

HNNGH

I'M SORRY, WHISPER...

YO-KAI ARE INVISIBLE TO THE HUMAN EYE, SO HE THINKS NATE DID IT.

WHY DID YOU INSPIRIT KATIE IN THE FIRST PLACE?

BECAUSE I WAS WORRIED ABOUT HER WALKING THROUGH HERE BY HERSELF.

I INSPIRITED HER SO WEIRDOS WOULD STAY AWAY.

REALLY? FOR KATIE?! THAT'S SO NICE!

...

HA HA. ♪

A FRIEND OF NATE'S IS A FRIEND OF MINE! ♪

WOW!

I DON'T BUY IT.

...

YOU GOT ME! I JUST WANTED TO SEE HOW YOU'D REACT!
BOW
HEY!
I KNEW IT.

## BONUS COMIC ③

# CHAPTER 228
# MOSQUITO YO-KAI SCRITCHY

BAAM
I'M NATE ADAMS. JUST AN ORDINARY ELEMEN-TARY SCHOOL STUDENT.
THE SAME BOY YOU SAW ON THE PREVI-OUS PAGE.

SKRCH
SKRCH
ITCHY, ITCHY, ITCHY, ITCHY!
ARRRRGH! MOSQUITOS!
SKRCH SKRCH
SKRCH SKRCH
NATE ADAMS
NATE! STOP!
GLARE
SCRATCHING WON'T HELP ANYTHING!
SCRATCHING WILL JUST CREATE SORES AND THEN YOU'LL BE IN EVEN MORE PAIN!
HALT
R-REALLY ...?
YUP...
NATE ADAMS

I...I HAVE FIRST-HAND EXPERIENCE...

Itch ouch... Itch ouch...

TWCH TWCH

TWCH TWCH

YOU'RE COVERED IN WOUNDS!

COULD IT BE?!
THAT'S STRANGE!
WE DON'T NORMALLY GET STUNG THIS BAD!

...

SO STUPID...
I FORGOT WE'RE OUT IN THE WILDERNESS!
I WAS ABOUT TO BLAME A YO-KAI!
WELL, ACTUALLY...

BUZZ

...IT IS BECAUSE OF A YO-KAI.

This guy.

WHAT?! IT IS BECAUSE OF A YO-KAI?!

A MOS-QUITO YO-KAI?! IT'S HUGE!

IF IT STUNG ME, IT'D SUCK ME COMPLETELY DRY!

HA HA HA, DON'T WORRY. ♪ I GOT TIRED OF BLOOD, SO I DON'T DRINK IT MUCH ANY-MORE, BUZZ. ♪

REALLY?

YEAH, I DON'T SUCK YOUR BLOOD...I JUST STING YOU! ♪ OVER AND OVER AGAIN! ♪

MOSQUITO YO-KAI SCRITCHY

THAT'S EVEN WORSE!

*What are you even doing it for?!*

IF YOU'RE NOT SUCKING OUR BLOOD, WHY DO YOU STING US...?

ITCHY ITCHY ITCHY ITCHY...

IF I STING YOU, IT MAKES YOU ITCHY, RIGHT?

I LOVE IT WHEN PEOPLE GET AGITATED BY AN ITCH THEY CAN'T GET RID OF! ♪
AHAHAHAHAH!
SO ITCHY! SO ITCHY! ♪
HE'S REALLY ANNOYING...
BUT ...

...PEOPLE SAY THEY FEEL ITCHY JUST FROM ME BEING AROUND. I WONDER WHY?

WEIRD...

GRR GRR GRR GRR GRR

JUST HIS PRESENCE MAKES PEOPLE FEEL ITCHY!!

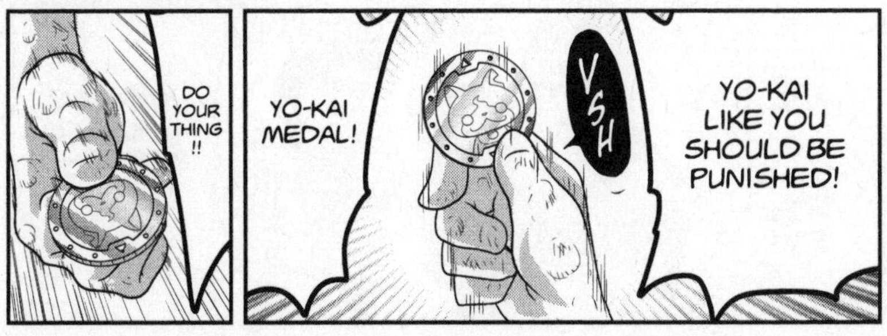

HUH?!

MY HAND'S SO SWOLLEN IT'S BLOCKING MY WATCH!

SQUEEE

WHAAAA?!

I'LL SLAP YOU WITH MY HANDS LIKE AN ORDINARY MOSQUITO!
DASH
YOU'RE GOING TO DO THE FIGHTING YOUR-SELF?!
SHFF
SHFF
TAKE THIS! AND THIS! AND THIS!
HE'S TOO BIG FOR THAT...
NAUGHTY NAUGHTY! I'LL TEACH YOU A LESSON!
SHUK
AHH! NATE!
SHUK

AHHHHH!!
PFFFFT
HEE HEE HEE. ♪ THAT'LL TEACH YOU TO SLAP PEOPLE! ♪
IT ITCHES, BUT NOW MY HANDS ARE BIG ENOUGH!
?!
WHAT...?! NO! YOU MEAN...YOU LET ME DO IT ON PURPOSE ?!
THAT'S RIGHT!

SLAP!

URRGH...

WOW! NATE DEFEATED A YO-KAI WITH HIS BARE HANDS!

NNGH...

IT'S NOT NICE TO MAKE PEOPLE ITCHY AND IRRITATED.

WHAT ARE YOU LECTURING ME FOR?

MAKING PEOPLE ITCH IS MY POWER...
SURE, BUT IT'S ALL ABOUT HOW YOU CHOOSE TO USE IT. ♪

WHAT IF YOU USED IT AGAINST PEOPLE TRYING TO DO SOME-THING BAD?
THEY'LL BE TOO ITCHY TO DO ANYTHING!
YOU CAN USE YOUR POWER TO ACTUALLY HELP PEOPLE! ♪
!!

HE'S GIVING ADVICE TO HIS ENEMY...

You could also use your power for...

...WHO CAUSED HIM SO MUCH TROUBLE...

What? More ideas ?!

HE'S...

BAAM

...AMAZING!

And, well... I guess that's it! ♪

WHAAAAA?

FIST BUMP
A WAY FOR A YO-KAI TO SIGNAL TO A HUMAN THAT THEY'VE OPENED UP THEIR HEART.
THIS RITUAL ALSO MAKES THE YO-KAI MEDAL, A SIGN OF FRIENDSHIP, APPEAR. ♪

THANK YOU! ♪ BUT DON'T PUSH YOURSELF TOO MUCH!

I'LL DO MY BEST TO HELP YOU OUT FROM NOW ON! ♪

IT'S GREAT TO MEET YOU! ♪

HURGH!

THUNG

KT

WHOOPS...

BE AWARE OF YOUR SURROUND-INGS AND ANY TROUBLE YOUR PRESENCE MIGHT CAUSE!
NO, IT'S MY FAULT...
TWCH TWCH
SORRY...I FORGOT MY HAND WAS SWOLLEN...
NATE ADAMS'S CURRENT NUMBER OF YO-KAI FRIENDS: 85

CHAPTER 229
PUNISHMENT YO-KAI VENOCT
THE BEST FRESH FISH
LIVE FISH
THE FISH PLACE
VRROOM

PAWS OF FURY !!
CAT YO-KAI
JIBANYAN
A CAT WHO BECAME
A YO-KAI AFTER BEING
HIT BY A TRUCK.

THU NG
MEEOOW!
SPLUBT

VRROOM
...
TWCH TWCH
HE WANTS TO BEAT A TRUCK AND PRACTICES FIGHTING THEM EVERY DAY.

HEY.
!
SHUP
ANOTHER DEFEAT, HUH?

VENOCT!!

VENOCT
A PUNISHER YO-KAI
WHO DOES NOT
ALLOW ANY EVIL.
A RANK S YO-KAI
OF JUSTICE.

W-W-W-WHAT ARE YOU DOING HERE?!
THE FI
...

SLAPT
HE PUNISHED ME RECENTLY. SO I HOPE HE'S NOT BACK FOR MORE...


SEE MORE IN VOL. 20.

I HEARD THERE WAS A YO-KAI PUNCHING TRUCKS IN THE AREA...
VEEN VEEN
W-W-WHY ARE YOU INTERESTED IN THAT YO-KAI?

WHY ...?

ANY YO-KAI THAT CAUSES TROUBLE FOR HUMANS IS A DISGRACE TO ALL OF US!

I WILL DEAL WITH THEM PERSONALLY!

THAT YOKAI! HAVE YOU HEARD OF THEM?

B-BMP

I, UHH... DUNNO, I...

...

...

BAM

HMM. HOW INTERESTING.

*I'm sorry I doubted you.*

HE BELIEVED IT!

*Is he really a Rank 5 Yo-kai?*

MEOW.
FRESH FISH
THE BEST FR
FRESH
I SEE. SO THAT'S WHY YOU'VE BEEN ATTACKING TRUCKS...
?
NO, I'M SORRY...
I'LL BE HONEST...

HEH.
THANK YOU FOR UNDERSTANDING!
I GUESS THERE'S A REASON FOR EVERYTHING.

I WILL NOT ACCEPT THIS! YOU HAVE AN UNJUSTIFIED VENDETTA AGAINST TRUCKS! IT'S UNFORGIVABLE!

WHAT?! I'M SORRY!

I JUST WANT TO BE STRONG!
PLEASE!
VENOCT! HELP ME TRAIN!
TRAIN?
I'M ABOUT TO TEACH YOU A LESSON!

OH, I SEE! YOU'RE SCARED I'LL BECOME STRONGER THAN YOU!
STAAARE
YOU'RE BEING TOO OBVIOUS! HE'LL NEVER FALL FOR...
...
HE-HE-HEH ...
JIBAN-YAN, WAS IT?

WHO ARE YOU CALLING SCARED?! I'LL SHOW YOU! I'LL TRAIN YOU TO BE STRONG AND THEN PUNISH YOU!

YES! I'LL MAKE YOU INCREDIBLY STRONG! PREPARE YOURSELF!

HE ACTUALLY FELL FOR IT...

*He's...maybe not that bright...*

ACTUAL FIGHTING IS THE BEST WAY TO TRAIN!

HERE I COME!

GLARE

SILENCE

...?

CHOMP
AGGGH!
No fair!
SHOCK
Ha!

YOU CALL THIS TRAIN-ING?!
HA! I DON'T EVEN NEED TO FIGHT YOU MYSELF!

JIBANYAN!
MNCH MNCH
M-MEOW... MEOW. I'M STUCK!
SHFF SHFF

OKAY, THEN ...

THE TWO DRAGONS AROUND VENOCT'S NECK ARE CREATED BY HIS AURA. THEY MOVE AT HIS COMMAND!

HRRRNGH--!
SHFF SHFF SHFF
ULPT!
YOU'RE GOING DEEPER?! WHAT ARE YOU THINKING?!
!!
TUG TUG
NO MATTER HOW STRONG SOMEONE IS, THEY CAN'T TOUGHEN THE INSIDE OF THEIR BODY!
THAT'S IT! ♪ EVEN A MONSTER IS HELPLESS AGAINST THE ENEMY INSIDE!
MEOW HA HA!
SHFF
GOOOOO!
HALT
?

HE'S STUCK IN THERE!

HELP... ME...

TWCH TWCH

WHEEZE

WHEEZE

I...I CAN'T BREATHE!

WHAT?

THE DRAGON CAN'T BREATHE EITHER!

HEEZE

...

...

WHAT A FOOL. HEY! SPIT HIM OUT.

HURRGH

SPLUB

NOW... LEFT DRAG-ON, GO!
...
...
...
WHAT ARE YOU WAITING FOR?! ATTACK!

SHF SHF SHF
...
JIBANYAN'S COVERED IN VOMIT, SO IT DOESN'T WANT TO GO NEAR HIM...
I don't blame it...
...
GLARE
SPLUBT
MEOW HA HA... NOW, YOU'RE SCARED TO EVEN TOUCH ME! I'VE FOUND TRULY INVINCIBLE ARMOR!
HE THINKS HE'S WINNING!
STAGGER
SHIING
NOW ...

SPLUB
SPLUB SPLUB
I'LL SIMPLY CATCH AND GRAB ONTO YOU! ♪
...!!
SPLUB
SPLUB
SPLUB
SHFF
SHF SHF
SPLUBT
YOU'RE NOT GOING ANY-WHERE!
JUUUMP
NOT A VERY HONOR-ABLE STRAT-EGY...
MEOW HAA!
...

SHA
MEEEOOW! THAT'S A DIRTY TRICK!
DIRTY? YOU'RE ABSO-LUTELY FILTHY.
!
MEOW ?
SIGH.
MEEEOOOW!

THWUNGK

OH.

SPLUBT

I HATE AUTOMOBILES.

YOU MUST NEVER FORGIVE THEM.

YES, SIR.

...

*IF YOU SEE A DENT IN A CAR OR TRUCK, IT MIGHT HAVE COME FROM A YO-KAI.*

CHAPTER 230
DOWNHEARTED YO-KAI NEGGPLANT
THE BEST FRESH FISH
LIVE FISH
FRESH
THE FISH PLACE
I'VE BEEN WORKIN' SO HARD TOO! DANGIT...
STAGGER STAGGER
SHF SHF
OH, GREAT. A DRUNK.
I CAN'T BELIEVE THE RESULTS...
SHIVER SHIVER
HUH?
HUH?
...

BAAAM
AN EGG-PLANT ?!

RRMBLL
OH...I GUESS YOU TWO HATE EGGPLANTS TOO?
HUH?

SHF SHF SHF
THE RANKINGS FOR KIDS' MOST HATED VEGETA-BLES!
HAVEN'T YOU HEARD ?!
WAIT... WHAT IS ALL THIS ?!
AMONG ALL OF THE VEGETA-BLES...
...EGG-PLANTS ARE RANKED ...

TA-DAAH

...EIGHTH!

WHAT ARE YOU EVEN TALKING ABOUT?!

Vegetables That Children Hate

| | | | |
|---|---|---|---|
| 1 | Brussel Sprouts | 6 | Asparagus |
| 2 | Green Pepper | 7 | Green Onion |
| 3 | Celery | 8 | Eggplant |
| 4 | Tomato | 9 | Carrot |
| 5 | Peas | 10 | Broccoli |

*According to our research.

I'M FLOORED...
SIIIGH
HEY...IF IT WAS FIRST OR SECOND PLACE, SURE, BUT EIGHTH PLACE IS NOTHING TO GET UPSET ABOUT!
...
GLARE
IS THAT SO?
WELL, I...

HAVE YOU EVER TOLD ANYONE THAT YOUR FAVORITE VEGETABLE WAS EGGPLANT?
HUH?!
N-N-NO...

WHAT DID I TELL YOU?! EVERYONE HATES EGG-PLANTS!
ARRRGH! WHAT'S EVEN THE POINT OF ANYTHING?!
THIS GUY NEEDS TO CALM DOWN...

EGGPLANTS ARE THE MOST HATED VEGETABLE IN THE WORLD!
I JUST CAN'T STAND IT. DANGIT...
IT'S JUST EIGHTH PLACE...

HEY, CHEER UP!
I BET YOU DON'T LIKE ME EITHER!
OH NO! I HATE ALL VEGETABLES! ♪
NOT JUST YOU! ♪
I'M A VERY FAIR CAT. I DON'T PLAY FAVORITES.
YOU THINK THAT MAKES ME FEEL BETTER?!

I REMEMBER NOW! THIS YO-KAI IS...
...NEGGPLANT!!
ONCE IT INSPIRITS YOU, YOU LOSE ALL SATISFACTION IN ANYTHING YOU DO!
AND YOU FEEL DEPRESSED AND NEGATIVE ABOUT EVERYTHING!
YOU JUST DON'T GET IT...
RRMBLL!!!

I JUST WANT YOU TO SAY GOOD THINGS ABOUT EGGPLANTS. I DON'T CARE ABOUT YO-KAI!
YAP YAP YAP YAP
KIDS AREN'T INTERESTED IN EGGPLANTS AND ARE EVEN LESS INTERESTED IN AN EGGPLANT YO-KAI...
SORRY...

OH! I LIKE GRILLED EGGPLANT! THOSE ARE GREAT! ♪
...

OOOH! THAT'S MORE LIKE IT!!
EGG-PLANTS ARE TRULY GREAT! ♪

KLAK-KLAK
I'LL TREAT YOU TO A GRILLED EGGPLANT RIGHT AWAY. ♪
KLAKKA KLAKKA
HOLD ON A MINUTE! HUMPH, HUMPH...
REALLY?!
THE BEST FRESH

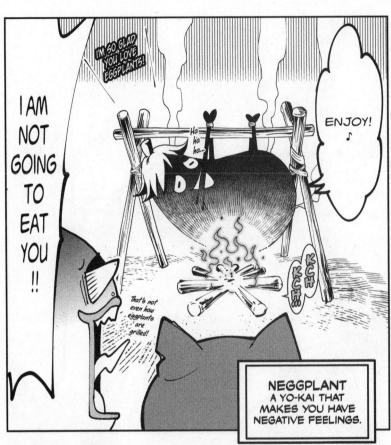

I'M SO GLAD YOU LOVE EGGPLANTS!

ENJOY! ♪

Ha ha ha...

I AM NOT GOING TO EAT YOU!!

KCH KCH KCH...

That's not even how eggplants are grilled!

NEGGPLANT
A YO-KAI THAT MAKES YOU HAVE NEGATIVE FEELINGS.

KRSHAAAA
IT'S SO HOT... HELP ME...!
HOTHOTHOT!
HOTHOTHOT!
THIS GUY IS A DISGRACE TO EGGPLANTS...

CHAPTER 231
WARRIOR YO-KAI SHOGUNYAN
THE BEST FRESH F
FRESH
THE FISH PLACE
SHOGUNYAN!
YOU HAVEN'T CHANGED AT ALL...
FWOOO
HNNGH
URGHH...
VRROOM
TWCH TWCH
JIBANYAN, I'VE BEEN WATCHING YOU AND YOUR ATTACKS ARE FAR TOO PREDICTABLE...
YOU NEED TO BE MORE ADAPTABLE.
FW8 FW8
SHOGUNYAN JIBANYAN'S ANCESTOR SPIRIT YO-KAI.
INTERESTING...
...
I SEE...
...

YOU CAN DO IT!

OKAY...BUT I WON'T GO EASY ON YOU JUST BECAUSE YOU'RE MY ANCESTOR!

ALSO ...

...YOU'RE NOT ALLOWED TO USE YOUR SWORD!

...

I'LL HELP YOU TRAIN!

WOW! TRAINED BY A LEGENDARY YO-KAI!

YOU EXPECT A SAMURAI TO FIGHT WITHOUT HIS SWORD?!
THAT'S NOT FAIR!
PLEASE!
LET ME USE IT!!
WHAT HAPPENED TO BEING ADAPTABLE?!
Have some self respect!

SHOOM SHOOM SHOOM SHOOM SHOOM
DID YOU FORGET? I'M A SPIRIT! YOUR PUNCHES CAN'T HARM ME!
OH NO!
WHEN I WANT TO FIGHT...
...I CAN INSPIRIT OTHER PEOPLE'S BODIES!
SHFF
MEOW?!
WHAT?! HE TOOK OVER JIBANYAN'S BODY!
IT FEELS GOOD TO HAVE LEGS AGAIN!
BAM
SAMURAI YO-KAI SHOGUNYAN
BUT...

BAAM
...NOW I DON'T HAVE ANYONE TO FIGHT AGAINST!
WHAT SHOULD I DO?
HOW DID HE NOT REALIZE THAT?
JIBANYAN'S BODY

NOW WE CAN'T BATTLE AT ALL!
WHAT A TERRIBLE BLUNDER! HOW COULD I?!
I HAVE NO CHOICE...

...BUT TO TAKE FULL RESPONSIBILITY BY COMMITTING SEPPUKU!
I'm sorry!
WAIT! STOP! YOU'RE OVERREACTING!
HA...
DON'T WORRY!

I'M A SPIRIT YO-KAI, SO I'LL BE FINE.

JIBANYAN'S THE ONLY ONE WHO WILL DIE. ♪

THAT'S EXACTLY WHAT I'M WORRIED ABOUT!

OH...

WELL, THEN...

...I'LL BORROW YOUR BODY TO FIGHT!
SWEEE
SHFF
MEOW?
WHAAAAT?!

YOUR BODY'S SO WRIGGLY, IT DOESN'T REALLY FEEL MUCH DIFFERENT THAN MINE.
WHISPER'S BODY.
UNGH...
WRIGGLE
WRIGGLE

YOU'RE NOT A SPIRIT, SO I CAN ATTACK YOU NOW!
PAWS OF...
...FURY!
ARRRRRGH!!
I DID IT. ♪

THAT WAS CLOSE! I GOT OUT AT THE LAST MINUTE!

TWCH TWCH

WHOOPS...

*Whisper...!*

HA HA! ♪

THIS WAS A BODY REPLACEMENT NINJUTSU!

NINJA TECHNIQUES?! YOU'RE A SAMURAI!

YOU JUST RAN AWAY!
I TOLD YOU—YOU HAVE TO BE ADAPTABLE. ♪
HNNGH
SOMETIMES RUNNING AWAY IS THE BEST OPTION!

CHAPTER 232
SEVEN GODS OF FORTUNE YO-KAI
FUKUROKUJU
FRESH FISH
FRESH
THE FISH PLACE
!
THAT... THAT'S ...!
BAAM
THAT... THAT'S ...!
...
HIS EARLOBES ARE MASSIVE!
RRMBLE
GULP...
RRMBLE...

FUKU-ROKUJU, ONE OF THE SEVEN GODS OF FORTUNE YO-KAI!
RIGHT! HE'S FRIENDS WITH EBISU! WHO WE MET BEFORE!
SEVEN GODS OF FORTUNE YO-KAI FUKUROKUJU
THEY SAY IT'S GOOD LUCK...
...TO TOUCH HIS EAR-LOBE!
WOW! THAT'S GREAT! ♪
HEY THERE! ♪ PLEASE ...
...
...LET ME...
SHF
YOUR ...
SHF
... TOUCH ...
SHF
... EAR-LOBE!
...

COME ON! JUST A LITTLE BIT!
PAWS OF FURIOUS EARLOBE TOUCHING!
YOU REALIZE HE'S A GOD, RIGHT?!
CHOOM
CHOOM
CHOOM
CHOOM
...!!
GRAB
I DIDN'T JUST TOUCH IT, I GRABBED IT!
That's gotta be good luck!
WOW! ♪
MEOW HA HA! ♪

WHAAAA?!
!!
SPROING
...
A GOD-LIKE PUNCH...!

GRRRP
I BET THE LONGER YOU HOLD HIS EARLOBE, THE LUCKIER YOU GET!
MEOW HA HA! ♪ I'M STILL HANGING ON! ♪

MEOW ?!
OH NO.
MEEOOOW!
TUUUG
HOW NOBLE! HE SAVED YOU EVEN THOUGH YOU WERE RUDE TO HIM!
THANK YOU SO MUCH!

MEOOW!

THUNCK!

FRESH

THE FISH PLACE

IT'S BETTER THAN BEING HIT BY A TRUCK...
HNNGH
...
MAYBE THAT'S THE GOOD LUCK YOU GOT FROM HIS EAR-LOBE! ♪
IT WASN'T... WORTH IT...
TWCH TWCH
YOU SHOULD APOLOGIZE TO FUKU-ROKUJU.

URGH ...
I'M SORRY ...

HUH?

...

HIS EAR-LOBE'S ALL STRETCHED OUT!
DANGLE
...

!

LOOK OUT! THERE'S A TRUCK COMING!

IF I TOUCH IT NOW, I BET I'LL HAVE EVEN BETTER LUCK! ♪

?

SWIP

MEOW HA HA! ♪ GOTCHA!

*The earlobe! It's mine!*

THU NG
EARLOBE
WOW! YOU GOT TO TOUCH IT WITH YOUR ENTIRE BODY!
TWCH TWCH
WHERE'S MY... GOOD LUCK...?
SO... UNFAIR...
YOU HAVE TO WORK HARD IF YOU WANT TO HAVE GOOD LUCK.

CHAPTER 233
IGNORANT YO-KAI LIFE-IS-PARFAIT
THE HEAT'S BROKEN AND THE WEATHER IS SO NICE! ♪
WONDER-FULLY REFRESH-ING! ♪
I JUST KNOW IT'S GOING TO BE A WONDERFUL DAY! ♪
FA LA LA ♪
HUH?

THE FISH PLACE
FRESH
LIVE FISH
BAAM
SOME GUY COVERED IN WOUNDS ON SUCH A REFRESHING DAY?!
SHUDDER

B-BMP B-BMP
ARE YOU OKAY?! ARE YOU EVEN ALIVE?!
OH!

...I DON'T WANT ANYTHING TO DO WITH IT! I'LL PRETEND LIKE I HAVEN'T SEEN ANYTHING! ♪
MY OH MY ooo
HOP

JIBANYAN, ARE YOU OKAY?! HANG IN THERE!
!!

I JUST IGNORED HIM, BUT THAT GUY'S TRYING TO HELP!

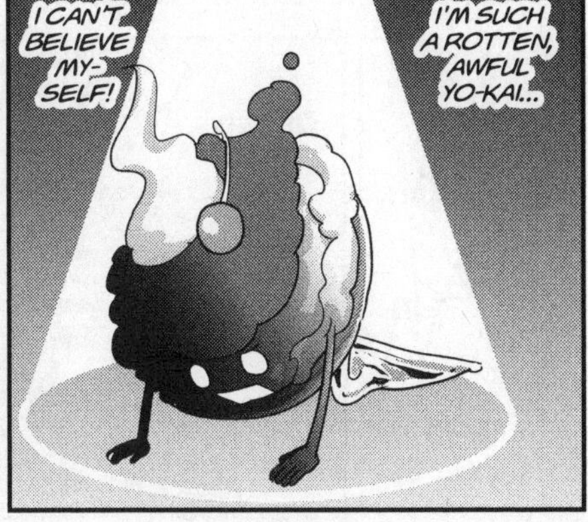
I'M SUCH A ROTTEN, AWFUL YO-KAI...
I CAN'T BELIEVE MY-SELF!

WELL, IT'S TOO LATE FOR ME TO DO ANYTHING NOW. I'LL LET THAT GUY TAKE CARE OF IT...

VROOM

ARGH!

NO!

The other guy got hit by a truck!

THIS TIME I HAVE TO HELP! WHAT KIND OF YO-KAI WOULD I BE OTHER-WISE?!


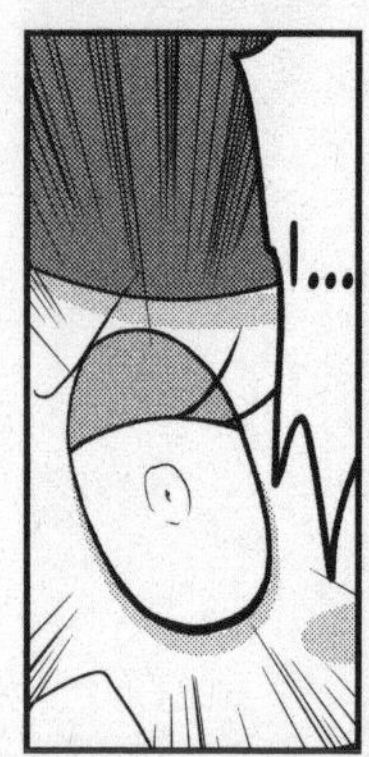

VROOM
BUT IF I DON'T GO HELP... THAT MAKES ME A TOTAL JERK!
VRRRR
BUT WHAT IF I GET HIT BY A TRUCK TOO?!

I DON'T CARE IF I'M A JERK!
DAASH
I'LL FIND A WAY TO LIVE WITH MYSELF AND MOVE ON!

IF YOU'RE READING THIS MANGA FOR THE FIRST TIME...
...PICK UP OUR OTHER GRAPHIC NOVELS TO FIND OUT WHY THIS CAT IS SO BEAT UP!
HEY, YOU!
!!
GULP

HOW COULD YOU JUST IGNORE SOMEONE WHO NEEDS HELP?! YOU'RE TERRIBLE!
SHOCK
TERRIBLE ?!

I CAN'T ARGUE. I DID TRY TO IGNORE HIM...
I HAVE NO CHOICE BUT TO...

...PRE-TEND LIKE I DIDN'T HEAR HIM AND LEAVE! ♪

AHH, WHAT A WONDERFUL DAY! ♪

THE FISH PLACE

FRESH FISH

IGNORANT YO-KAI
LIFE-IS-PARFAIT

SHE'S A YO-KAI WHO FEIGNS IGNORANCE!
EVEN SO, I CAN'T ACCEPT THIS!
BUT YOU CAN'T FORCE PEOPLE TO BE HELPFUL ...
...

!!
THIS IS FOR YOUR OWN GOOD! YOU CAN'T JUST RUN AWAY FROM THINGS YOU DON'T LIKE!

HE...
HE'S THE FIRST PERSON WHO'S EVER TRIED TO SCOLD ME LIKE THAT!

BAAM
...SEEMS LIKE AN ANNOYING GUY! I'LL JUST IGNORE HIM!
...
SHF SHF

HEY! COME BACK HERE!
QUIT BOTHERING ME!

OH NO!

WHY DID I TURN BACK? WHY DIDN'T I JUST IGNORE HIM...?
IS...IS WHAT HE'S SAYING GETTING THROUGH TO ME?!
...

W-WHAT?
HUH?

ARRRRRRRGH!

VRROOM

THERE'S A TRUCK COMING.

# CHAPTER 234
# WAITING FOR THE OPPORTUNITY YO-KAI LIE-IN HEART

...DON'T WANT ANYTHING!
BAAAM
THEN LEAVE! YOU'RE WASTING OUR PRECIOUS PAGE SPACE WITH DRAMATIC REACTIONS!

...

BAAAM

NO! YOU'RE NOT DOING A GOOD JOB!

GOOD JOB AT WHAT?!

VSH

THAT'S MORE LIKE IT!

WHAT'S MORE LIKE IT?!

THE TIMING OF YOUR REACTION WAS PERFECT!
THE TIMING ...?

THE FIRST TIME, YOU REACTED TOO EARLY. YOU SHOULD HAVE WAITED A LITTLE LONGER BEFORE SHOUTING "THEN LEAVE!!" AT ME.
YOUR REACTION WAS TOO LONG TOO.
...
LIVE FISH


THE MOST IMPORTANT THING IN BATTLES, IN REACTIONS ...

...AND IN EVERY-THING ELSE IS TIMING!

YOU MUST BE PATIENT AND WAIT FOR THE PERFECT MOMENT TO MAKE YOUR MOVE!

DAAM
THAT'S WHAT IT MEANS TO WAIT FOR THE RIGHT MOMENT!
I'M A YO-KAI WHO TEACHES PEOPLE THE IMPOR-TANCE OF TIMING!
...
I'VE FINISHED EXPLAINING THINGS TO YOU, SO THE TIME HAS FINALLY COME FOR ME TO REVEAL MY IDENTITY. MY NAME IS...

MEOW ...
GOOD LUCK NEXT TIME.
HEY! PAY ATTENTION!
LIE-IN HEART !!
WAITING FOR THE OPPORTUNITY YO-KAI
LIE-IN HEART
...
...
...
YOU STILL DON'T GET IT, DO YOU?
MEOW.
...
I'M SORRY. YOU WERE TAKING SO LONG WE MOVED ON.
...
WHAT DO YOU WANT?
OKAY!
LET'S HEAD HOME.
TMP TMP
HEY! COME BACK!
...AND EVERYONE WILL BE PREPARED TO LISTEN TO YOU!
WAITING LIKE THIS WILL DRAW EVERYONE'S ATTENTION...

THE POINT IS—YOUR ATTACKS ARE POORLY TIMED.

YOU JUST CHARGE AT THE ENEMY! YOU NEED TO WATCH THEIR MOVEMENTS.

POORLY TIMED ATTACKS ...?

YES! YOU'RE FINALLY GETTING IT! THE TIME HAS COME!
BAAM
IF YOU WISH, I CAN TEACH YOU ABOUT PROPER TIMING IN BATTLE!

WHAT? YOU'RE GOING TO TRAIN ME?

THAT'S RIGHT.
I'LL SHOW YOU THE IMPOR-TANCE OF WAITING FOR THE RIGHT MOMENT.
KRCH
A SWORD?! THAT'S NO FAIR!
DON'T WORRY. I WON'T ...

...USE ANY PUNCHES OR KICKS!
BAM
I'D RATHER YOU NOT USE THE SWORD!

THAT REACTION WAS PERFECT!
TOP NOTCH! I LOVED IT!
WHAT?! I'M BEING SERIOUS! DON'T USE THE SWORD!

YOU HAVE TO WATCH YOUR OPPONENT AND WAIT FOR THE MOMENT TO MAKE YOUR MOVE.
WATCH MY OPPONENT ...
GULP

...
AREN'T YOU GOING TO DRAW YOUR SWORD?

I'M WAITING FOR THE RIGHT MOMENT.
FEEL FREE TO ATTACK.
...
JIBANYAN, HE'S TRYING TO TRICK YOU!
I KNOW.

...

I HAVE A FEELING THAT WHOEVER MOVES FIRST WILL LOSE.

I SEE YOU'VE REALIZED THE IMPORTANCE OF WAITING.

BUT LET'S SEE IF YOU CAN BEAT ME IN WAITING FOR THE RIGHT MOMENT TO ATTACK.
RRMBLL

FWOOO

N-NOT YET...
FEEBLE
WAIT... I MUST WAIT...
ATTACK ALREADY! HOW LONG ARE YOU GOING TO WAIT?!
SHIVER SHIVER
TWCH TWCH
SHUDDER SHUDDER
I CALL THIS BATTLE A DRAW...
FWUMP
MEOW...I THINK IT'S THE RIGHT MOMENT TO SAY THAT...
WHAT TOOK YOU SO LONG ...?
HNNGH
IF YOU WAIT TOO LONG, YOU'LL MISS OPPORTUNI-TIES. BE CAREFUL!

CHAPTER 235
ADVENTURE LOVER YO-KAI WONDERNYAN
UNLIKE NORMAL CHAPTERS, TODAY WE'RE GOING ON AN ADVEN-TURE!
MY NAME ISN'T JIBANYAN ...

BAM
IT'S WONDER-NYAN!
WONDERNYAN
A YO-KAI WHO LOVES ADVENTURE.
WE'LL DISCOVER AN UNCHARTED ISLAND AND CREATE JIBANYANLAND!
YEAH!
WE CAN CREATE NATE-LAND AND WHISPER VILLAGE TOO! ♪
JUST A VILLAGE ?!
SPLOOSH
LET'S GO! ♪

I LOVE ADVEN-TURES! ♪ THEY'RE SO FUN AND EXCITING! ♪

YEAH!♪

KRCH

SUCH A CARE-FREE ATTI-TUDE COULD COST YOU YOUR LIFE ON AN AD-VENTURE!

KRRKT
THE WINDS BROKE THE MAST!
AHH!
FWOOSH
NO! THE SAIL'S BLOW-ING AWAY!
WHY DIDN'T IT HOLD?!
KRRSHAA
WHOA! A TIDAL WAVE!
WHAT TERRIBLE LUCK!
SHWAAA
ABORT! ABORT MISSION!
IT'S TOO EARLY FOR THAT!
WE HAVE TO STAY CALM!
YOU'RE RIGHT! WE HAVE TO REMAIN CALM EVEN DURING THE MOST DIFFICULT SITUA-TIONS!!

I'M SURE THINGS WILL WORK THEMSELVES OUT. ♪
FWUMP
YOU'RE BEING TOO CALM! WE HAVE TO DO SOMETHING!
THERE, THERE. HAVE SOME TEA, YOU TWO. ♪
SHFFF
Don't get mad. ♪
A TEA SET?! COULDN'T YOU BRING SOMETHING MORE USEFUL?!
HUH?
IS THAT...
OH.

IT'S A SHARK!

SHOCK

SHAAA

WHOA!

FIRST THE FORCES OF NATURE AND NOW A WILD BEAST! THIS IS A REAL ADVENTURE!

TALK ABOUT CAREFREE!

USE THE YO-KAI WATCH AND CALL FOR HELP!!

THIS IS AN ADVENTURE! SHOULDN'T WE FIND A WAY TO SOLVE THINGS OURSELVES?!

RIGHT, JIBANYAN?!

FORTUNATELY, I PUT ALL MY MEDALS IN MY BAG!

GREAT THINKING!

I HOOKED IT TO THE MAST, SO...

UHH...THE MAST AND SAIL GOT WASHED AWAY PAGES AGO.
That means your bag too...
BLUB BLUB BLUB
SHOOCK
NOOOOO!
My medals!
...

I'LL GO AND GET THE BAG!
BUT THERE'S A SHARK SWIMMING AROUND US!
YOU'LL NEVER MAKE IT!
ARE YOU JUST GOING TO WAIT UNTIL THE SHARK GIVES UP?!

WHAT'S THE POINT OF GOING ON AN ADVEN-TURE...
SHA
...IF YOU'RE NOT WILLING TO TAKE MATTERS INTO YOUR OWN HANDS?!
CALL FOR HELP!
I GUESS HE CAN STILL GET THINGS DONE WHEN HE HAS TO...
YEEAAAAH!
SPLISH SPLOSH
HE'S SWIMMING SO FAST!
SHWAA

SHASHASH
BUT THE SHARK CAUGHT UP WITH HIM IMMEDIATELY!
SHOCK
OF COURSE! IT'S A SHARK!
SHWAAAA
...
AHHHH!
*Help me!*

...
IF I HAD THE MEDALS, I COULD CALL A YO-KAI THAT CAN-
IF ONLY THERE WAS A YO-KAI WHO COULD FLY!

I TOTALLY FORGOT THAT I CAN FLY!
AHHHHH!
GO HELP JIBANYAN! HURRY!
So ridicu-lous...
SPLOSH
I GOT YOUR BAG...
WOW! YOU GOT AWAY FROM THE SHARK!
FWUMP
...
QUICK! CALL SOME-ONE!
I CAN'T SUMMON A FRIEND INTO SUCH A DANGER-OUS SITUATION...
...
I CAN FLY, AFTER ALL!
THEN I'LL DO SOME-THING ABOUT IT!
!
I MAY NOT HAVE THE POWER TO DEFEAT A SHARK, BUT...
SUUUCK

FWOOOM
WE CAN GET OUT OF HERE ON THE WHISPER BALLOON!
WOOOW.♪
COME ON, NATE! ♪

SILENCE

HRRRNG! NNNGH!

Y-Y-YOU'RE TOO HEAVY FOR ME!

HEEEY!

SHAAA

SHAAA

HE'S JUST FILLED UP WITH NORMAL AIR, AFTER ALL...

You can do it!
DANGLE
I'M THE BAIT ?!
YOU'RE GOING TO FISH FOR THE SHARK ?!
DON'T WORRY, I'LL GIVE YOU ALL THE CREDIT! ♪
WAIT! STOP!
DANGLE DANGLE
I'VE GOT A BAD FEELING ABOUT THIS!
SPLOOOSH
AIYEEEEE!
WHISPER!
GOTCHA!

OUT-SIDE THE WATER, YOU'RE ALL MINE!
PAWS OF FURY!
PLIP
THAT'S WHAT YOU WERE PLANN-ING!
YOU SHOULD THANK WHISPER. ♪
IT WORKED, WHISPER. ♪
HUH?

OH NO! I LET GO OF THE OAR!

PLIP

BLUB BLUB BLUP

TWCH TWCH

*YO-KAI WATCH* VOLUME 21 END! / CONTINUED IN VOLUME 22

# VENOCT

RRMBLL
I'VE BEEN SHOWING UP IN THE MANGA A LOT RECENTLY...
THE MANGA ARTIST PROBABLY LIKES YOU, VENOCT.
PUNISHMENT YO-KAI VENOCT
IT IS UNACCEPTABLE THAT HE GETS TO CHOOSE WHICH YO-KAI APPEAR MORE OFTEN JUST BASED ON HIS LIKES AND DISLIKES.
Totally unfair.
IT CAN'T BE HELPED. WHEN HE DRAWS HIS FAVORITE CHARACTERS...
RRMBLL
...HE GETS FIRED UP AND THE FINAL PRODUCT IS BETTER. ♪
I DON'T CARE WHAT HE FEELS. HE SHOULD BE PUNISHED.
CLENCH
EH, ACTUALLY ...
...IT'S PROBABLY JUST BECAUSE YOU'RE POPULAR, VENOCT. ♪
R-REALLY ?
THAT SHUT HIM UP QUICKLY !!
And he doesn't seem that upset about it, either...

# AUTHOR BIO

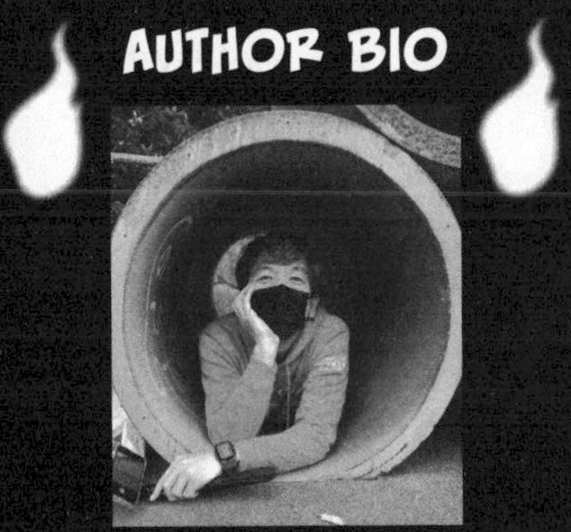

I hardly read manga these days. But I used to read a lot when I was a child.

I read about ten series.

I decided to become a manga artist after reading those ten works. Sometimes people say "Your manga is a rip-off of that one manga..." and it's some series that I haven't even read before.

Cover Illustration: Noriyuki Konishi

**Noriyuki Konishi hails from Shimabara City in Nagasaki Prefecture, Japan. He debuted with the one-shot *E-CUFF* in *Monthly Shonen Jump Original* in 1997. He is known in Japan for writing manga adaptations of *AM Driver* and *Mushiking: King of the Beetles*, along with *Saiyuki Hiro Go-Kū Den!*, *Chōhenshin Gag Gaiden!! Card Warrior Kamen Riders*, *Go-Go-Go Saiyuki: Shin Gokūden* and more. Konishi was the recipient of the 38th Kodansha manga award in 2014 and the 60th Shogakukan manga award in 2015.**

# THIS IS THE END OF THIS GRAPHIC NOVEL!

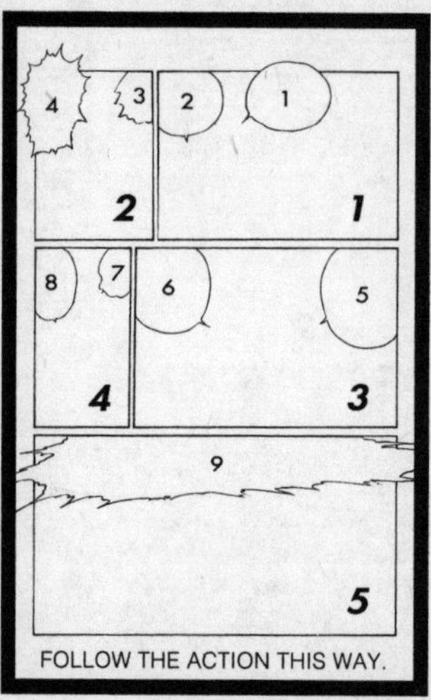


**To properly enjoy this graphic novel, please turn it around and begin reading from right to left.**